AMULET OF AVANTIA

→ BOOK NINETEEN ←

NIXA
THE DEATH BRINGER

BEAST QUEST®

AMULET OF AVANTIA

→ BOOK NINETEEN ←

NIXA
THE DEATH BRINGER

ADAM BLADE

ILLUSTRATED BY EZRA TUCKER

SCHOLASTIC INC.

New York Toronto London Auckland
Sydney Mexico City New Delhi Hong Kong

With special thanks to Cherith Baldry

For Miroslav Torak with all good wishes

ISBN 978-0-545-27214-8   4547 1975   4/11

Beast Quest series created by Beast Quest Ltd., London.
BEAST QUEST is a trademark of Beast Quest Ltd.

12 11 10 9 8 7 6 5 4 3 2 1   11 12 13 14 15 16/0

Designed by Tim Hall
Printed in the U.S.A.   40
First printing, April 2011

Beast Quest

Amulet of Avantia

#19: Nixa the Death Bringer

#20: Equinus the Spirit Horse

#21: Rashouk the Cave Troll

#22: Luna the Moon Wolf

#23: Blaze the Ice Dragon

#24: Stealth the Ghost Panther

⊷ TOM ⊷

PREFERRED WEAPON: Sword and Magic Shield

ALSO CARRIES: Destiny Compass, Jewel Belt

SPECIAL SKILLS: Over the course of his Quest, Tom has gained many special items for his shield giving him protection from fire, water, and cold, extra speed in battle, protection from falling from heights, and magic healing ability. He also has the powers he gained from the Golden Armor, giving him incredible sight, courage, strength, endurance, sword skills, and energy.

⭢ Elenna ⭠

PREFERRED WEAPON: Bow & Arrow

ALSO CARRIES: Nothing. Between her bow and her wolf, Silver, Elenna doesn't need anything else!

SPECIAL SKILLS: Not only is Elenna an expert hunter, she is also knowledgeable about boats and water. But most important, she can think quickly in tight spots, which has helped Tom more than once!

⇥ STORM ⇤

Tom's horse, a gift
from King Hugo.
Storm's good instincts
and speed have helped
Tom and Elenna from
the very beginning.

⇥ SILVER ⇤

Elenna's tame wolf and
constant companion. Not
only is Silver good to have
on their side in a fight,
but the wolf can also help
Tom and Elenna find
food when they're hungry.

ADURO

The good wizard of
Avantia and one of Tom's
closest allies. Aduro has
helped Tom many times,
but when Aduro was
captured by Malvel, Tom
was able to help the good
wizard by rescuing him.

MALVEL

Tom's enemy, determined
to enslave the Beasts of
Avantia and defeat Tom.
This evil wizard rules over
Gorgonia, the Dark
Realm. If he is near,
danger is sure to follow.

All hail, fellow followers of the Quest.

We have not met before but, like you, I have been watching Tom's adventures with a close eye. Do you know who I am? Have you heard of Taladon, the Master of the Beasts? I have returned — just in time for my son, Tom, to save me from a fate worse than death. The evil wizard, Malvel, has stolen something precious from me and until Tom is able to complete another Quest, I cannot be returned to full life. I must wait between worlds, neither human nor ghost. I am half the man I once was and only Tom can return me to my former glory.

Will Tom have the strength of heart to help his father? Another Quest can test even the most determined hero. And there may be a heavy price for my son to pay if he defeats six more Beasts. . . .

All I can do is hope — that Tom is successful. Will you put your power behind Tom and wish him well? I know I can count on my son — can I count on you, too? Not a moment can be wasted. As this latest Quest unfolds, much rides on it. We must all be brave.

Taladon

FARMER GRETLIN STOOD AT THE EDGE OF HIS wheat field. Two days ago, the wheat had stood waist high, shining golden in the sun. Now it was dull gray, almost black, and a damp, musty smell came from it.

"This is worse than the time the crops were scorched by fire," Gretlin muttered to himself. "Is Errinel under threat again?"

Gretlin strode out into the wheat field, pushing aside the gray, dying stems. He was desperately searching for any patches that were still untouched by this evil blight. At the opposite side of the field the wheat was still golden, but most of his crop had been destroyed.

The harsh rays of the morning sun slanted down, dazzling Gretlin as they struck something on the ground. Shielding his eyes, the farmer bent down and saw a strange metallic object half-buried.

As he reached to pick it up, the wheat rustled around him, though there was no wind. The stalks curved and swooped, like dozens of arms trying to hold him back.

Confused, Gretlin backed away from the metal object. The wheat hissed and thrashed around him. "It's alive!" he whispered, turning to flee.

He pushed his way through the writhing stalks of wheat to the edge of the field, then halted as he heard a voice carried on the breeze. He pressed his hands to his ears as the sound slashed at them like a razor.

Looking to see where the voice came from, Gretlin spotted a woman at the opposite side of the wheat field, where the crop still grew tall and strong. She was slender, with long golden hair; she wore robes of scarlet silk that floated out around her as she walked toward the farmer. She cast handfuls of glittering dust over the wheat, and where it fell the golden stalks shriveled and turned gray. Around her feet were the still bodies of other villagers, slumped on the ground.

"Hey!" Gretlin shouted. "Stop that!" Angrily, he began to run toward the woman, waving his arms above his head. "Get away from my wheat!"

The woman glided up to him, her bare feet hardly touching the ground. She held out her hand. A strange silver object with a sliver of blue enamel rested on her open palm. It looked like the thing Gretlin had seen half-buried in the field.

Squinting in the sunlight, Gretlin could see that it was a piece broken off from something bigger. He could just make out faintly etched marks on one side. Then he gaped in astonishment as he realized that the scrap of metal wasn't resting on the woman's hand — it was floating just above it!

"Who are you?" Gretlin asked, his voice hoarse with fear. *Surely she can't be human!*

"My name is Nixa." The woman's voice was soft and beautiful.

But as she spoke, the bright morning sky changed to a threatening purple. Clouds swallowed up the sun. The purple faded to black.

"What's happening?" Gretlin gasped.

The air vibrated with a sound like thunder. As the farmer stared in horror, the woman began to change. Her arms split and became a mass of thrashing tentacles. Her two eyes divided into a cluster of bulging, glistening spheres. Her scarlet robes dissolved and her body sagged into a thousand wrinkles. Green slime seeped out and dripped onto the ground. Gretlin choked on the foul stench that flooded around him.

"My name is Nixa," the monster repeated. Her voice still sounded like a beautiful chime of bells, but it stabbed Gretlin's ears like a knife. He clapped his hands to his ears and felt blood spurting between his fingers.

Farmer Gretlin screamed as a mass of tentacles reached out toward him.

CHAPTER ONE

A FATHER RETURNS

"ONE HUNDRED AND FIFTY-ONE! ONE HUNDRED and fifty-two!" Captain Harkman's voice echoed across the training courtyard.

Tom groaned as he pumped his arms in yet another push-up. He thought he was going to die of boredom, if he didn't first melt into a puddle under the hot sun of Avantia.

He remembered how he had returned from Gorgonia a few weeks before, fresh from the Quest where he had defeated the evil wizard Malvel for the third time.

"Avantia owes you a great debt," the king had

said. *"Tom, you may choose any position you like in my court. Ask, and it's yours."*

"Thank you, sire," Tom had replied. *"I'd like to be a soldier in your army."*

He'd thought that would be fun, and a great way to go on helping Avantia. *But I was wrong*, he sighed to himself. What was the point of doing push-ups all day long when he had powers that the cadet officer, Captain Harkman, had never dreamed of?

I made a mistake, Tom muttered to himself as his arms pumped up and down. *I wish there was something else I could do. Maybe another Quest . . .*

He snatched a glance across the courtyard to where his friend Elenna was teaching archery to the youngest cadets. He watched her positioning one boy's fingers on the bowstring, and saw his face break into a delighted grin as his arrow thumped home.

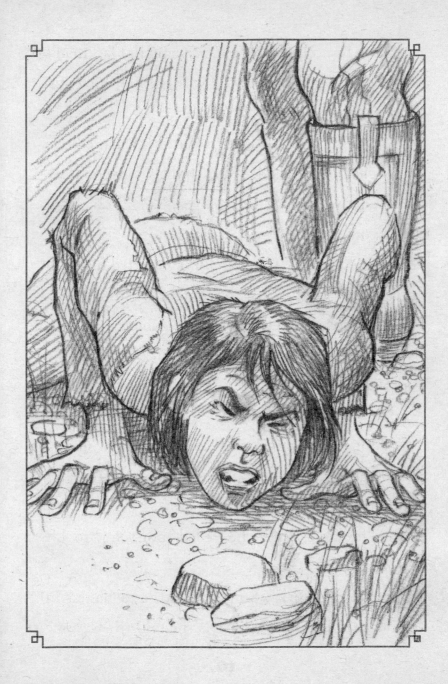

Tom heard heavy footsteps. Captain Harkman's feet halted beside him; he was tapping his whip against his polished riding boots.

"Slacking again?" Captain Harkman snarled. He crouched down beside Tom, so that Tom could see his red, sweating face and gingery hair. "You're just like your father. He was a slacker, too."

Fury flooded through Tom. He gritted his teeth together with the effort of controlling his temper.

"Taladon trained here once, when he was a young man," the captain went on, straightening up. "I was glad to see him go. He was lazy, and arrogant, too. He was —"

Tom heard the sound of an arrow whizzing through the air. It just missed Captain Harkman's head as he ducked and rolled away.

"Who fired that?" he yelled, bouncing to his feet again.

Elenna ran over, bow in hand, and halted in front of the captain. "Sorry," she said. "It was one of my cadets. He hasn't quite gotten the hang of archery yet."

Tom hid a smile. He knew perfectly well that Elenna had fired the arrow herself. Just because they weren't on a Beast Quest didn't mean that he and Elenna wouldn't watch each other's backs anymore.

A voice called out from the palace gardens. "He has returned! Taladon the Swift has returned!"

Tom froze. *Taladon? My father?*

Breathlessly, he scrambled to his feet and pounded toward the archway that separated the training courtyard from the gardens, weaving his way around his fellow cadets.

"Hey! You there! Come back!"

Tom ignored Captain Harkman's shouts. He didn't care how the captain would punish him, if only he could see his father.

He heard light footsteps racing behind him. He knew who that would be — Elenna.

Bursting through the archway, Tom saw one of

the king's messengers dashing across the gardens. "He's here!" he yelled. "Taladon has returned!"

Tom took the steps up to the main palace door three at a time. The guards by the open doors waved him through and he ran down the long corridor that led toward King Hugo's throne room.

My father left when I was a baby, he thought. *Am I really going to see him now?*

Dashing around a corner, Tom came to a halt. The throne room doors were open and a man was stepping through them. The sun slanting through a nearby window outlined his broad shoulders and long, black cloak. He strode forward confidently, his head held high.

"Father!" Tom sprang toward him, but the man didn't seem to have heard. He walked on without looking back, and the guards pulled the throne room doors closed behind him.

"Father?" Tom repeated to himself, standing alone in the corridor.

CHAPTER TWO

MAN OR GHOST?

"WAS THAT TALADON?" ELENNA PANTED AS she caught up with Tom outside the throne room.

"I . . . I'm not sure." Tom's heart was thumping hard at the glimpse of the tall man.

"There's only one way to find out," Elenna said, nodding at the closed doors of the throne room.

The guards pushed the doors open again and Tom hurried forward with Elenna at his side.

Inside, King Hugo sat on his throne with his court magician, Wizard Aduro, standing beside him. But they didn't look as happy as Tom had expected. The good wizard's face was pale, and King Hugo's eyes were wide with shock; his hands gripped the arms of his throne so hard that his knuckles were white. The king's courtiers stood around, whispering uneasily.

Sudden fear seized Tom. He stumbled to a halt. The knight he had seen in the corridor was kneeling in front of King Hugo. "Father?" Tom asked.

The knight rose to his feet and turned. He was a tall man with a thatch of hair, a curling brown beard, and deep-set brown eyes. He wore a travel-stained tunic and leggings, covered by a dusty black cloak.

"I can see he's your father," Elenna whispered. "He looks just like an older version of you."

The knight looked at Tom and held his gaze; Tom could not look away. He waited for the flood of emotions, but . . . nothing happened. *Shouldn't I be glad to see my father?* he thought. Somehow this wasn't how he had imagined their first meeting.

The knight smiled. "My son," he said. His voice sounded rusty, as if he hadn't used it in a long time.

Elenna nudged Tom. "Go on!"

Dazed, Tom stumbled forward to give his father a hug. But when he tried to wrap his arms around Taladon, they passed right through, as if his father was no more solid than a wisp of cloud.

A gasp came from the king's courtiers and Tom heard Elenna stifle a cry. Wizard Aduro whispered something to King Hugo, and the king waved a hand at his followers. "Leave us," he ordered. "Everyone except Aduro, Tom, and Elenna."

As the courtiers and the guards filed out, glancing nervously at Tom and his father, Tom stepped back. Icy shivers were running through his body. Taladon was looking down at him, his eyes filled with love and sadness.

"What's happened?" Tom gasped. "Are you a ghost? Are you *dead*?"

Aduro crossed the throne room to shut the doors behind the last of the courtiers. Returning to the king's side, he stopped beside Taladon. He raised one hand; a glittering mist flowed from his fingers and wrapped Taladon in its silver coils. Then it returned to Wizard Aduro and vanished.

Aduro bent his head as if he was listening. "Taladon lives," he said at last, "but he is stranded between the real world and the spirit world. Taladon, has this anything to do with the Ghost Beasts?"

Taladon nodded.

"Ghost Beasts?" Tom felt more confused than ever. "What are *they*? I've never heard of them."

"Sit down, Tom." Taladon pointed to a footstool at the bottom of the steps leading to the throne. "Aduro and I will tell you everything."

Tom went to the footstool and sat down. Elenna fetched a second stool and sat down next to him. Tom was glad that she was there.

Wizard Aduro swept his wand through the air. White fire flared out of it and formed a glowing circle in the middle of the throne room.

"Keep your eyes on that," Aduro instructed Tom and Elenna, "and you will see what has happened to Taladon."

"And the Ghost Beasts?" Elenna asked. "I thought we destroyed all the Beasts in Gorgonia."

"Malvel's most deadly Beasts have yet to be revealed to you. They don't live in Gorgonia," Wizard Aduro told her solemnly. "They are here, in the darkest corners of Avantia."

"Here!?" Tom exclaimed, his stomach churning.

King Hugo nodded, his eyes troubled. "I had hoped that they would never rise to trouble Avantia again," he murmured. "That's why we never told you about them, Tom."

"The Beasts live in the Forbidden Land," Aduro went on.

Tom and Elenna exchanged a startled glance.

"What's the Forbidden Land?" Elenna asked. "I've never heard of it."

"Few of the people of Avantia know of it," Aduro told her. "A wall surrounds it to keep them out. It is dangerous to set foot there."

"Because of the Ghost Beasts?" Tom said.

"Yes," the wizard told him. "They thrive on its shadows and gloom. No normal man can touch them, but they can cause the worst destruction you can imagine. They have no body to risk losing. So they can take risks that even a normal Beast would think twice about." His voice grew harder and his eyes flashed. "Tom, I hope you can be brave. These are the most dangerous Beasts yet!"

→ CHAPTER THREE ←

A NEW QUEST

TOM FELT A SPARK OF EXCITEMENT. WAS THIS the beginning of a new Quest?

Taladon stretched out a hand toward the magical screen. The silver fire died, and Tom saw a picture of a rocky hillside. An armored knight was there, his sword in his hand. Tom recognized the golden armor that belonged to the Master of the Beasts.

The knight raised his sword high above his head, ready to bring it down on a beautiful golden-haired woman dressed in scarlet robes.

"Is that *you?*" Tom asked his father, growing confused. "Fighting someone who isn't even armed?"

"Watch," Taladon said.

The knight brought his sword whistling down, but it passed right through the woman's body, just as Tom's arms had passed through Taladon. At the same moment the woman began to change. Her arms sprouted tentacles, and her beautiful face became hideously wrinkled, with a cluster of staring eyes.

Elenna drew in her breath sharply. "Is that a Ghost Beast?"

Taladon nodded. "That is Nixa the Death Bringer. She is a deadly Beast who can take the shape of anything she wants. But her voice is always beautiful."

Tom shuddered. Somehow the idea of a beautiful voice made Nixa seem more evil than ever.

On the screen Taladon and the woman battled each other, the monster's tentacles wrapped around the armored body of the knight.

"Was it Nixa who trapped you between the worlds?" Tom asked.

Taladon shook his head. "Aduro armed me with the precious Amulet of Avantia," he replied.

"What's that?" Elenna's voice was filled with curiosity.

"It's a disk of blue and silver carved with powerful symbols," Aduro answered, stroking his beard. "I made it to protect the Master of the Beasts against the ghosts."

"And it served me well, until . . ." Taladon stretched out his arm and the picture of the battling knight and the monster faded. The magical screen darkened, as if it were filled with a swirling black cloud. Then the cloud cleared, and a familiar figure began to take shape. Tom recognized the black robes, the cruel features shadowed by a black hood, and the sunken eyes glittering with evil. A mocking laugh echoed through the darkness.

"Malvel!" Tom exclaimed, jumping to his feet as anger swelled inside him. "It was Malvel who stranded you between the worlds!"

"It was." Taladon's eyes narrowed and his mouth set in a hard line; Tom could tell that his father shared his anger. "I battled five of the six Ghost Beasts: Nixa the Death Bringer, Equinus the Spirit Horse, Rashouk the Cave Troll, Luna the Moon Wolf, and Blaze the Ice Dragon."

"What about the sixth?" Elenna asked. There was awe in her voice as she heard the names of the fearsome Beasts Taladon had conquered.

"The sixth was Stealth the Ghost Panther." Taladon paced across the throne room, turned sharply, and pointed once more at the magical screen.

Tom sat down again to watch. The image of Malvel faded, to be replaced by a rocky hillside. On the topmost pinnacle a panther with three tails was perched. Its body was long and sleek. Its eyes were green like jade. As Tom stared in fascinated horror, the Ghost Beast leaped into the air, its muscular body blotting out the sun.

It looked fiercer than any Beast Tom had ever faced.

"You fought *him*?" Tom breathed out, his gaze returning to his father. *Taladon must be the bravest man in the world!*

His father nodded. The picture on the screen blurred and formed again. Now Tom saw the Ghost Panther hovering over the crest of the hill while Taladon, still wearing the golden armor, slashed his sword at his outstretched claws and ducked to avoid the Beast's snapping fangs. For the first time, Tom noticed that his father wore a silver disk on a chain around his neck. There was a circle of bright blue in the center of the disk.

The sky was split by a bolt of black lightning. It struck Taladon in the chest and he staggered back as the silver amulet shattered into pieces and spun away in glittering fragments.

Tom choked back a cry when he saw

Stealth swooping down on his father. But the Beast's swiping paws passed straight through Taladon's body.

"The lightning made you a ghost!" Tom exclaimed.

"It was Malvel's lightning," Taladon replied. "The Dark Wizard knew the Beast could not kill me, so he changed his plan. After I was struck by the lightning, I was a prisoner of Malvel's magic for a long time. Longer than I care to recall."

The magic screen showed Tom and Elenna a sphere of surging gray cloud, shot through with flashes of glittering black. Taladon, without his armor now, floated helplessly in the middle of it.

"What happened then?" Elenna asked.

Taladon gestured at the screen and the cloudy ball faded. His body drifted to the ground; he seemed to be in the middle of a flat plain under a threatening purple sky.

"That's Gorgonia!" Elenna said, glancing at Tom.

Taladon nodded. "Suddenly, I was free. I started to walk across the plain, until I saw a shimmering archway leading into Avantia. I was able to escape Gorgonia and come back here, and I still don't know why."

Aduro, who had been standing by the king's throne as he listened to the story, strode forward again and thumped his staff on the floor. "That was the moment when Tom defeated Malvel for the third time," he explained. "And any magic, good or evil, grows weak if it has been repelled three times. Your son freed you, Taladon."

Taladon's gaze rested on Tom, his eyes warm with gratitude. "Thank you," he said quietly.

Tom's heart swelled with pride, but a moment later his anger surged back. He clenched his fists. "I'll make Malvel pay for what he's done to you!"

Looking puzzled, Taladon turned to Wizard Aduro. "I still don't understand *what* Malvel has done to me. Why am I a ghost?"

"And is he going to stay like this forever?" Elenna added anxiously.

"The black lightning must have robbed you of your powers and trapped you between the worlds," Aduro said thoughtfully. "But if the pieces of the amulet can be found and put back together, you will become the man you once were."

Tom and Elenna both leaped to their feet. "Then we have to find the pieces!" Tom exclaimed.

Wizard Aduro looked from Tom to Elenna and back again, a faint smile on his face. "You both have great courage," he said, "but it's not that simple. The amulet was broken into six pieces, and each is now guarded by a Ghost Beast. You can only restore your father if you defeat all the Beasts and put the amulet together again as one. Remember, the Beasts will do everything in their power to keep the pieces from you, and may hide them if they have to. This Quest will be your biggest test yet."

Tom's stomach lurched as he thought of the two deadly Beasts he had seen on the magic screen, and remembered the others that Taladon had named. Even with his magical powers, could he hope to defeat all the evil creatures?

But Tom didn't hesitate. Saving Taladon was more important than anything. He hadn't waited so long for his father to return only to have him still so far away.

"This will be our next Quest," he said firmly.

Wizard Aduro and King Hugo exchanged a smile.

Elenna stood at Tom's shoulder, her eyes bright with determination. "Just tell us where we have to go," she said.

"Very well." Wizard Aduro inclined his head. "Avantia's two champions will leave first thing tomorrow morning."

Tom's whole body tingled with excitement. Taladon was back — in a way — and Tom had a new Quest.

This one will earn me the greatest prize I've ever won, he thought. *My father will be restored.*

→ Chapter Four ←

A BRUSH WITH HOME

Leading Storm by the reins, Tom walked across the training courtyard on his way out of the palace. His sword hung from the jeweled belt around his waist, and his shield was fastened onto Storm's saddle. The stallion's hooves rang out in a rapid pace on the paving stones.

"I think Storm's as anxious to set out on our new Quest as we are," Tom remarked.

Storm blew noisily through his nose as if he were agreeing.

Silver, the gray wolf, was padding along beside Elenna. He waved his tail enthusiastically.

"You're ready, too, aren't you, boy?" Elenna asked, giving him a pat on the head. "You'll help us defeat the Ghost Beasts."

"Pick your feet up there!" Captain Harkman's shout made Tom look around. "Call yourselves soldiers?"

The young cadets Tom had trained with were jogging around and around the courtyard with packs on their backs. All of them were stumbling with exhaustion, their faces streaming with sweat.

"That makes me feel bad," Tom muttered guiltily. "I'm supposed to be with them."

"Not anymore," Elenna said with a grin.

Tom headed for the gates.

"Hey, you! Stop!" Captain Harkman strode across the courtyard, waving his riding whip. His face was red and his ginger mustache bristled. "Where do you think you're going?" he demanded. "Why didn't you report for training this morning?"

"I'm on important business for the king," Tom explained.

The captain snorted. "Don't lie to me. Do you think I was born yesterday? Go and get your uniform on *now*, or you'll be sweeping out the barracks for the next week!"

Tom hid a smile. Digging into his pocket, he brought out the scroll King Hugo had given him the night before. He held it out to Captain Harkman. "Perhaps this will explain, sir," he said politely.

As the captain unfastened the scroll, Tom exchanged a glance with Elenna.

The captain's gaze traveled swiftly over the scroll. His eyes bulged and his face grew redder than ever. "Official business . . . freedom of the realm . . . King Hugo's seal," he spluttered.

With a final snort he shoved the scroll back into Tom's hands and returned to the group of cadets, who were taking the chance to have a well-earned rest. Most of them were trying hard to suppress laughter.

"What's so funny?" Captain Harkman roared. "Get a move on! Ten times around the courtyard, and I want to see you *run!*"

Tom and Elenna carried on toward the palace gates. Tom felt his spirits rising. There would be no more training with Captain Harkman. He was at the start of another Beast Quest. There would be challenges ahead of him, but he would do all he could to find the pieces of the amulet and bring Taladon back into the real world.

While there's blood in my veins, he thought, *I'll save my father!*

"Which way do we go?" Elenna asked. She and Tom were both riding on Storm, with Silver bounding alongside. The city walls lay behind them and the road they were on led through rolling green hills. "I'd never heard of the Forbidden Land until yesterday."

"I had," Tom said, drawing Storm to a halt. "But I'm not sure where it is. That's why Wizard Aduro gave us the map." He stretched out one hand. "Map!" he called commandingly.

A grin spread over Tom's face as a patch of shimmering silver appeared, bobbing in the air in front of him. He almost felt like Wizard Aduro, able to call things up out of thin air. The silver patch was a little like the magic screen Aduro had conjured the day before to show them the story of Taladon. When Tom reached out to touch it, his fingers went right through it.

"I suppose it makes sense," he murmured. "A map for finding Ghost Beasts would have to be ghostly."

Lines began to appear on the glimmering surface of the map, showing the familiar outline of Avantia with its hills and rivers, roads and towns. But in the south and east of the kingdom, a new stretch of land revealed itself. Letters scrolled out across it: *The Forbidden Land.*

"There!" Elenna exclaimed, peering over Tom's shoulder. "That's where we've got to get to."

Tom watched as more letters appeared inside the Forbidden Land. They were small and cramped and he had to peer closely at the map to make them out.

"The Dead Valley of Avantia," he said, suppressing a shiver. "That must be where we'll find the first Ghost Beast."

Tom and Elenna rode Storm swiftly through the hills of Avantia, bypassing villages and crossing rivers. The sun shone, and a brisk breeze was blowing.

As the sun began to go down, Tom slowed to a normal speed again. "Well done, boy," he said to Storm, leaning forward to pat the stallion's glossy black neck. "We've come a long way today."

"I know where we are!" Elenna cried, pointing due south to where Tom could just make out smoke rising from the huddled rooftops of a village. "Isn't that Errinel?"

Tom nodded. He hadn't meant to pass so close to his home, but it lay near the most direct route to the Forbidden Land. He couldn't resist using the special sight from his golden helmet, so that he could see it more clearly. He felt as if he were a bird, flying just above the main street until he came to the forge where his uncle and aunt lived. He saw his aunt Maria come out of the house with a basket on her arm, and hurry down the street toward the local market. Through the open door of the forge, Tom could see his uncle Henry beating out metal with a hammer.

"Do you want to visit?" Elenna asked. "We could spend the night with your aunt and uncle."

For a moment Tom was tempted. His home looked so welcoming; they could sleep in a real bed, and eat one of Aunt Maria's delicious suppers. Best of all, he would see his family again.

"No," he sighed at last. "They would ask too many questions. It's best not to get distracted when we're on a Beast Quest. And how would I explain that Father is back — as a ghost?"

Tugging on the reins, he urged Storm along the road, with his back to Errinel and his face set toward the Forbidden Land.

Out there, a Ghost Beast was waiting for him.

CHAPTER FIVE

DOUBLE TAKE

THE ROAD TRAVELED IN A LONG LOOP AROUND
Errinel, then rose in a gradual slope to a gap
between two hills. The land beyond the ridge fell
away more steeply, with patches of dense woodland
on either side of the road.

"We ought to make camp soon," Elenna
suggested. "I can catch us something for supper."

"Good idea," Tom replied. "You should be able
to find something among the trees over there." He
pointed to the nearest woods.

Elenna slid down off Storm's back, unfastened
her bow and arrows from his saddle, and jogged

off toward the woods, quickly disappearing among the trees.

"I'll find some grass for Storm to eat!" Tom called after her.

Elenna vanished into the thicket.

Tom got down from Storm and led him along the road. As he passed the woods, he noticed several rabbits feeding. When they heard Storm's hooves they sprang up and bounded into the undergrowth.

"Elenna's sure to catch us a good supper," Tom said to Silver.

The gray wolf let out a yelp of agreement and dashed off to catch his own food.

Tom continued down the road until he reached a spot where a spring welled up out of the ground between two jutting rocks. Lush grass grew all around the pool.

"There you go, boy," Tom said as he unsaddled the black stallion and let him wander off to graze.

Tom splashed his face with water from the spring, and took a long drink from his cupped hands. He was resting and watching Storm chomp the grass when he heard footsteps behind him.

Tom turned to see Elenna striding down the road toward him. She still carried her bow, with her quiver of arrows slung over one shoulder, but Tom couldn't see any rabbits. Her mouth was set in a grim line and she was pale.

Tom sprang to his feet. "What's the matter? Where's our supper?"

Elenna threw her bow and arrows down beside the pool. "I couldn't find anything," she replied. "Not even a rabbit."

"But I saw —" Tom broke off. The look on Elenna's face stopped him. Something had obviously happened to make her unhappy, and he didn't want to upset her any more.

"We ought to keep moving," Elenna snapped.

"All right." Tom's stomach was grumbling with hunger, and the sun was already low on the horizon, casting long shadows from the nearby woods across their path. They wouldn't be able to travel much farther before it was dark. But he knew Elenna must have a good reason for wanting to keep going.

She'll talk to me when she's ready, Tom thought. But he couldn't ignore the prickle of unease that traveled up his spine.

"Silver went into the woods," Tom said as he picked up Storm's saddle. "He'll come if you call."

Elenna shrugged. "He'll catch up to us."

Tom gave his friend an uneasy look. It wasn't like her not to care whether her animal friend was with her or not. "Right. Let's head for the Dead Valley," he said.

He saddled Storm and led him along the path. Elenna retrieved her bow and arrows and walked beside them. Before they had gone very far, she asked, "Do you know anything about the Forbidden Land? It sounds really frightening."

Tom felt a stab of surprise. Elenna hardly ever admitted to being afraid of *anything*! "Uncle Henry used to tell me and my friends about it, in Errinel," he began, casting another glance at Elenna. "No one from Avantia is supposed to go there anymore. The legends say it used to be beautiful and prosperous, but then the evil Beasts made it their home."

Elenna shivered. "I don't think I want to go there!"

Tom could hardly believe she'd said that! "Uncle Henry said that something evil had brought the touch of death to it," he went on. "Now it's walled off from the rest of Avantia. We'll have to —"

"Tom! Tom!"

A familiar voice behind him froze Tom in his

tracks. He turned, his heart almost stopping as he saw Elenna racing down the path toward him!

But Elenna's right beside me! Tom whirled back to glance at his friend, who had stopped when he did and turned to look back. *There are two of them!*

CHAPTER SIX

THE SOUND OF EVIL

TOM GRIPPED HIS SWORD AND DREW IT OUT of its sheath. Now he remembered what Wizard Aduro had told him: The Ghost Beast Nixa was a shape-shifter! She could appear in any form she wanted to.

I can't believe I've been so stupid! Elenna isn't scared of Quests . . . and she never fails at hunting. And she would never leave Silver behind!

"You're not Elenna!" he shouted at the figure by his side. His hand trembled as he struggled to aim his sword at someone who looked like his friend. "You're Nixa the Death Bringer!"

"No!" The Elenna beside him stepped back, raising her hands to protect herself. Her eyes were wide with terror and her face twisted in an ugly grimace. "You've got it wrong, Tom! I'm the real one. . . . *She's* Nixa!"

"Tom!" the other Elenna called out, pounding even faster down the path to reach them. "Defeat her now! She's Nixa!"

Tom looked from one to the other, his sword stretched out in front of him. His hand shook with the agony of deciding. He *had* to confront the Beast, but he couldn't risk hurting Elenna, not if there was even the slightest doubt as to who was the real one.

"I can't be sure. . . ." he whispered.

The Elenna at Tom's side stepped forward and grabbed the other Elenna as she reached them. She whirled her around until Tom wasn't sure who was who anymore. They were both dressed in the same clothes, with the same untidy hair, and the same smudge of dirt across their foreheads. They carried the same bows and arrows.

I don't know! screamed a voice inside Tom's head.

Tom heard furious yelps coming from the direction of the woods. Silver was charging across the grass, his strong legs pumping. Reaching the road, he hurled himself at the Elenna nearest Tom, all the hairs on his back bristling with anger.

"Clever boy!" Tom exclaimed. "The Ghost Beast can't fool you!"

The fake Elenna staggered back as Silver crashed into her. "Get off, you flea-bitten animal!" she cried.

Her shape flickered and changed into the form of the beautiful woman in scarlet silks that Tom had seen on Aduro's magical screen. Silver passed right through her and landed on the path beyond with a whimper of sheer astonishment.

Gripping his sword, Tom faced Nixa. She had two ways to attack, he realized. When she was flesh and blood, she was strong but could be injured, but in this ghost form, no one could touch her.

But I have to try, he thought.

Tom swung his sword wildly — too wildly. The tip caught on a boulder, dragging across the surface of the stone with a harsh, grating sound.

A deep shudder passed through Nixa. Her face set into a grimace of fear and loathing. Tom stared as slime broke out all over her body, her eyes multiplied, and she became the tentacled monster that had attacked his father.

Silver crouched beside her, growling, while Storm let out a startled whinny and backed away rapidly.

Nixa shrank back, then turned and fled down the road.

"What's happening?" Elenna asked, coming to stand beside Tom. "What's the matter with her?"

"It was the *sound*," Tom replied, watching the space where Nixa had been. "She hated the sound my sword made on the rock. Now I know how to defeat her!"

A blue light shone out behind him, casting his and Elenna's shadows ahead of them.

Tom whirled round. A man stood in the shimmering light: his father, Taladon. He still looked weak and ghostly.

Surprise flooded over Tom. He hadn't expected to see his father again until his Quest was completed.

"You're lucky to be alive," Taladon said. "You shouldn't get too close to Nixa."

"But she ran before we could even fight," Tom replied. "How can I defeat her if I'm not to get close to her?"

"She has a weapon you don't know about yet. I'm here to warn you: Be careful of her voice," his father told him.

"You said her voice is beautiful," Elenna said, frowning. "How can it be dangerous?"

"Beautiful and deadly," said Taladon. "It feels like a dagger of ice, piercing your ears and your heart. Few who hear it live. Take care, Tom. If you let Nixa get too close to you, she will use her voice. If your sword hadn't caught on the boulder, all of you could be dead by now. Nixa is a Beast who lives and dies through heart-wrenching sounds. . . ."

Taladon's voice began to die away, and the shimmering blue light faded.

"Wait!" Tom exclaimed. "I want to ask . . ."

But Taladon had vanished.

Silver, who had stayed crouching on the ground while Taladon was speaking, got up, gave himself a shake, and trotted over to Elenna. She ruffled his fur and he pressed close to her side.

Tom walked over to where Storm was standing, and patted the stallion's neck. "Come on, boy. We've got to find Nixa now, and get the piece of the amulet before she does any more harm."

Tom swung himself onto Storm's saddle and held out a hand to help Elenna up behind him.

"Nixa shouldn't give us too much trouble; now we know what frightens her," Elenna said as they set off along the road once more.

"I'm not so sure," Tom said. An unpleasant thought sent shivers of apprehension down his spine. "She ran away from the noise, but what was she doing here in the first place? The Ghost Beasts are supposed to stay in the Forbidden Land — but Nixa dared to come out and meet us right here, in the middle of Avantia. What else will she dare to do?"

CHAPTER SEVEN

A TOUCH OF MAGIC

"LOOK! OVER THERE!" TOM REINED IN STORM as he and Elenna emerged from a belt of trees. Ahead of them lay a high gray wall, stretching away into the distance and barring their way. "That must be the Forbidden Land."

"How are we going to get in?" Elenna asked, peering over Tom's shoulder. "We'll never be able to climb that."

"There must be a way," Tom said, urging Storm forward again.

As they drew closer, Tom could see that he was right. The road led up to an arched opening in the wall. Two heavy wooden gates studded with brass nails blocked the way.

Tom jumped down from his horse and pushed at the gates. To his surprise, they swung open easily, and he, Elenna, and the animals passed through them.

Tom pushed the gates closed again and looked around. Behind him lay the rich fields and woods of Avantia, but all the land on this side of the wall was gray and dead. There was no movement and no sound except for the whistling of wind. A gray haze covered the sky.

"I can't believe we're still in Avantia," Elenna said with a shiver.

"The Ghost Beasts have made this happen." Tom clenched his fists. Now that he saw the Forbidden Land for himself, he was even more determined to fight the Beasts. No part of Avantia should be like this!

The road wound ahead through stony hills. Tom climbed back onto Storm and urged him forward.

"This should take us to the Dead Valley," he said, remembering what he had seen on Wizard Aduro's magic map. "That's where we'll find Nixa."

They traveled under the blank gray sky as the darkness spread by the minute. Storm's hooves threw up clouds of dust, stinging Tom's and Elenna's eyes, and making them cough. Silver padded along with his head down and his tongue lolling.

The road began to climb steeply until it reached a rocky plateau. Huddled shapes were scattered across the flat surface. Silver bounded up to the nearest one and sniffed at it. Then he raised his head and let out a mournful howl.

"Something's wrong!" Elenna's voice was full of anxiety.

Tom guided Storm over. Horror crept over him when he realized it was the body of a man, lying facedown with his arms wrapped around his head as if he was trying to protect himself. He didn't look like a citizen of Avantia — his skin was as gray as the land around them.

These people must live in the Forbidden Land, Tom thought. Aduro hadn't told him that anyone survived here.

"I think he's dead," Elenna whispered.

Silver looked up, whining miserably, and Storm shied away, refusing to come any closer.

Tom leaned forward to pat his neck. "Steady, boy. We need to find out what happened, and then we'll be on our way."

He slid down from the saddle and Elenna followed. As he bent over the body, Tom could see that Elenna was right: The man was dead.

"Nixa must be close," he murmured. "This man hasn't been dead long."

"Look — blood." Elenna pointed to dark, sticky pools on either side of the man's head.

"He bled from the ears!" An icy shiver ran down Tom's spine.

"Nixa must have used her voice," Elenna said nervously.

Looking around, Tom could see now that the other shapes were bodies, too, all of them with dusty, gray skin. They seemed to form a trail leading across the plateau.

"At least it should be easy to track Nixa down," Tom said grimly.

They mounted Storm again and set off, following the trail of bodies. The men and women seemed to have tried to cover their ears. They all had the telltale pools of blood beside their heads. Two of the bodies were dogs, who had died with their legs stretched out as if they had been trying to leap on Nixa.

The sight of the bodies only made Tom more determined to defeat the Beast. *Somehow I have to stop her!* he thought.

At last, they arrived at a gaping hole in the rocky hillside. A tunnel led into the hill; Tom caught a glimpse of wooden posts holding up the roof.

"This must be an old mine," he said.

"Nixa might be in there," Elenna suggested. "It would be a good hiding place."

"I think you could be right," Tom said.

Tom tried to suppress the chill that raced through him. "There'll be echoes in the mine," he went on. "Nixa's voice will be even louder. We need something to protect our ears."

Elenna jumped down from Storm and cautiously approached the entrance to the mine. Tom dismounted, summoning all the magical strength of heart that he could gain from his golden chain mail. But even with its power, he wasn't sure he could force his feet to carry him into the mine where Nixa was lurking. If he and Elenna heard the Ghost Beast's evil voice, they would face certain death.

"But I have to try," he muttered to himself. "My father is depending on me."

Resolutely, he turned toward the gaping entrance to the mine. But before he could step forward, a shimmering blue light sprang up between him and the dark hole. This time, it was the form of Wizard Aduro that took shape there.

"Well done, Tom." The wizard's voice sounded clearly inside Tom's head. "No one in Avantia will ever doubt your courage. But a little magic never did any harm."

He raised his hands and blue light streamed from his fingertips. It formed into tendrils that touched Tom and Elenna on both ears. Tom started as he saw Elenna's lips move, but he couldn't hear a thing!

"I have enchanted your ears," Aduro explained, his voice sounding inside Tom's head. "You will be protected for a little while. But inside the mines my magic is weak. Once you go in there, it will start to fade. You will not be protected for long, so you must hurry!"

Tom and Elenna exchanged a glance and nodded vigorously.

"Good luck!" Aduro said as the blue light began to fade.

When the wizard vanished, Tom turned to Storm and unslung his shield from his saddle. "Wait here, boy." It felt strange to speak and not hear the sound of his own voice. "We'll be back soon."

Elenna crouched beside Silver, stroking the thick fur on his neck. Tom couldn't hear what she was saying to the wolf, but a moment later she straightened up and gestured toward the entrance of the mine.

Tom drew his sword and led the way into the darkness.

CHAPTER EIGHT

INTO THE CAVE

THE LIGHT FROM THE ENTRANCE DIED AWAY
behind Tom and Elenna as they ventured cautiously
through the tunnel. Tom couldn't see anything.
He guided himself by touching the wall with his
free hand. He could feel Elenna close behind him,
her hand on his shoulder.

Before they had gone very far, Tom began to
feel a tingling in his feet, and in the fingers that
touched the tunnel wall. The walls and floor were
vibrating!

"Nixa must be using her voice against us," he
said before he remembered that Elenna couldn't

hear him. *But it's not going to work*, he thought. *We're much smarter than she is!*

Gradually, Tom could make out the tunnel stretching out in front of him. A faint light trickled in from somewhere up ahead. As he and Elenna walked forward, the light grew stronger until they came out into a wide-open space. Thin shafts of weak light tumbled down from gaps and crevices.

Stalactites hung from the roof of the cave, while stalagmites grew up from the floor. Tom thought they looked like rows of huge misshapen teeth.

Elenna prodded Tom sharply in the back and pointed to the other side of the cave. Tom braced himself as he caught a glimpse of a monstrous creature weaving her way in and out of the stalagmites. He recognized the coiling tentacles and skin dripping with slime.

Nixa!

Tom could see the Ghost Beast's lips moving, and knew that she was using her deadly voice. But he couldn't hear a thing. With Elenna just behind him, he darted from one stalagmite to the next, trying to stay hidden as he made his way toward the Beast.

But Nixa spotted them. Her clumps of eyes bulged with rage.

She knows we can't hear her, Tom thought.

Nixa's huge mouth gaped wide as if she was letting out a shriek. A fierce wind whipped through the cave; Tom and Elenna grabbed the nearest stalagmite so the blast wouldn't sweep them away.

The wind ripped chunks of rock from the stalactites and stalagmites, and sent them hurtling toward Tom and Elenna. Tom grabbed Elenna and dove for cover behind the stalagmite.

"Coward!" he yelled. He couldn't hear himself, but he knew Nixa would hear him. "Come closer and fight me!"

Tom managed to unsling his shield in time to ward off the first of the rocks. *This is so strange*, he thought. He could feel the thump of the rocks as they hit his shield and bounced off, and see them crashing to the cave floor, but he couldn't hear a sound. *It's like a dream, as if it isn't really happening.*

As he crouched, Tom could feel the vibrations in the floor and the stalagmite growing stronger. *Nixa's getting louder — or Aduro's magic is starting to fail.*

Tom knew he had no time to waste. Springing up, he charged straight at Nixa, whirling his sword above his head.

But before he reached the monster, Nixa swiftly changed her shape. She became the beautiful woman in the scarlet robes.

"For Avantia!" Tom yelled out his battle cry, even though he couldn't hear himself. He struck Nixa with all his strength, but passed right through her, just as he had passed through Taladon back at the palace. She'd changed into her ghost form.

Tom gritted his teeth with fury. *We'll have to outwit her, not outfight her.*

He spun around. Nixa stood in front of him, her head thrown back as she laughed. In one hand she held up a broken piece of silver decorated with a sliver of blue enamel.

Tom tensed as he recognized part of the Amulet of Avantia. If he could get it, he would be one step closer to saving his father.

While there's blood in my veins, I will not fail!

CHAPTER NINE

STRENGTH OF THE SWORD

TOM REMEMBERED HOW NIXA HAD RUN AWAY when he scraped his sword against the rock by the side of the road. *That's it! We have to use sound to defeat her!*

Darting to the nearby wall of the cave, Tom scraped his sword across it. Though he couldn't hear the noise, he saw sparks flying out and chips of rock scattering everywhere.

Nixa's beautiful face took on a look of horror. Her mouth gaped wide, and Tom felt the vibrations of her scream drilling at his ears.

We haven't got long!

He stepped forward to face Nixa again. The Ghost Beast, her eyes wild with fear, swept forward and straight through him. She was heading for the mouth of the cave, where Tom and Elenna had entered.

We can't let her escape! Tom thought as he took off after her.

Elenna was standing in Nixa's way. She gripped one of her arrows and drew it down the side of one of the stalagmites.

"Well done, Elenna!" Tom yelled.

His friend started, alarmed, as if she'd heard something. But Tom couldn't worry now about the enchantment fading. Turned back by the sound from Elenna's arrow, Nixa was rushing straight for him.

Tom drew his sword across the stone floor of the cave, and Nixa halted once again. Trapped between Tom and Elenna, she was starting to panic. Her mouth gaped as she kept on screaming.

This isn't working, Tom thought as he scraped his sword again. *She can't get away, but I can't defeat her.*

The vibrations in the cave floor were growing stronger, and it was hard for Tom to keep his balance. His ears were starting to hum with a dull pain; across the cave he saw Elenna shaking her head uncomfortably, as if she could feel it, too. Wizard Aduro's enchantment was fading. Soon they would be forced to listen to Nixa's deadly voice.

"I've got to do something!" Tom exclaimed aloud, trying to shut out Nixa's screams. "It's now or never!"

Tom summoned the power of his magical boots and leaped at Nixa. His confidence surged back as he felt the magical golden armor boosting him high into the air. As he came down, he scraped his sword against the wall of the cave, to make an earsplitting noise. The Ghost Beast backed away from the sound, but Tom landed right beside her, passing through the outer folds of her scarlet robes with the force of his landing.

Tom made a grab for the piece of the amulet. Nixa snatched it away from him, and as Tom grabbed for it again she shifted into the form of the many-eyed monster dripping with slime. One set of tentacles lashed around Tom's waist, and with another tentacle she held the silver fragment high out of Tom's reach.

Struggling against Nixa's fierce grip, Tom managed to bend over and drag his sword across the rocky cave floor.

Nixa's tentacles uncoiled and she threw Tom against the wall of the cave. He slumped to the ground, his vision blurred and the breath driven out of him. When he could get up, he saw Elenna with her bow out, firing arrow after arrow into Nixa's slimy body.

The Ghost Beast bellowed with rage as she tugged the shafts out and flung them aside. The low hum in Tom's ears grew louder, and pain stabbed sharply into his head. Nixa was charging across the cave, straight at Elenna.

No! Scrambling to his feet, Tom dropped his shield and leaped upon Nixa. He knew he had to use the noise of his sword to destroy her, before all the enchantment was gone. He grabbed one of her tentacles, digging his fingers into the slippery surface, and wrenched her around to face him. At the same moment he scraped his sword down the nearest stalagmite — close enough to Nixa for the sound to terrify her.

Nixa let out a furious shriek. The pain of her voice made Tom let her go, and, dropping his sword, he clapped his hands over his ears. He felt as if daggers were stabbing deep into his head.

Elenna had fallen to her knees. She was trying to shut the sound out, too, her arms wrapped around her head. She exchanged an agonized glance with Tom.

In a daze of pain, Tom grabbed his sword again and dragged it across the floor one last time. The Ghost Beast's scream was abruptly cut off. Her monstrous body seemed to swell, then exploded in a shower of slimy fragments. They spattered over the cave walls and floor, letting out a foul smell.

The piece of the amulet fell to the floor. Tom ran to it and picked it up, holding it over his head in triumph.

Yes! I have the first piece!

Elenna ran over to Tom. "You did it!" she exclaimed. "That was amazing!"

Tom laughed. It was good to hear his friend's voice again. "We did it together," he said.

Tom fitted his sword into its sheath and rubbed the scrap of the amulet on his tunic to get rid of Nixa's slime. It shone with a watery gleam in the fading light from the roof.

Meanwhile, Elenna crossed the cave to retrieve the arrows she had shot at Nixa. "They're all covered in slime," she said. "That Beast was disgusting!"

As Tom waited for her, he realized that a shimmering blue light was growing behind him. He spun around to see his father smiling at him.

"Well done, both of you," said Taladon. "Tom, you make me proud."

Tom held up the piece of the amulet. "Look, I rescued the first piece."

Taladon nodded. "So I see. I can feel my strength beginning to return already. I know I won't be a ghost forever — not with you to help me." Tom could see that his father's shape already looked stronger, as if life was flowing back into him.

Tom's heart swelled with pride, but at the same time a faint uneasiness touched him like icy fingers. *I feel weak. What's wrong with me?*

Elenna hurried to join Tom and his father, a bunch of arrows in her hand. "What happens now?" she asked.

"You must find the next piece of the amulet," Taladon told them. Already his ghostly form was starting to fade. "It's in the keeping of Equinus the Spirit Horse."

"We won't fail you!" Tom called out as his father vanished.

With Elenna beside him, he headed into the tunnel, toward the mouth of the cave. This time they pushed on quickly through the darkness until they could see the gray light of the Forbidden Land shining ahead of them.

Tom called on his magic powers to leap forward, eager to see Storm and Silver again. But somehow he lost his balance as he took off, and stumbled to his knees against the tunnel wall.

"Are you hurt?" Elenna asked anxiously. "Tom? What's wrong?"

Tom shook his head. For a moment the breath was driven out of his body. "I'm fine," he gasped. "I just took off badly. That's all."

But I still feel weak, he thought to himself. *Something's wrong. . . .*

He tried to push his suspicions out of his mind, but he couldn't stop wondering why he had failed to summon enough power for his leap.

He led the way out of the tunnel. This wasn't the time to start worrying. They had to step out again into the Forbidden Land, and track down Equinus the Spirit Horse, wherever he might be.

Whatever happens, Tom told himself, *I'll bring my father back to his human form!* Another Quest was waiting for them.

Tom's Quest Continues with . . .

BeastQuest®

Amulet of Avantia

⇥ Book Twenty ⇤

EQUINUS

The Spirit Horse

Read a Sneak Peek Here!

A NEW DANGER

Tom MADE HIS WAY THROUGH THE MINE tunnels with Elenna close by his side. He could see daylight ahead. Only moments before they had defeated Nixa the Death Bringer, one of Malvel's evil Ghost Beasts, and he was glad to be leaving the dark and the memories of the shape-shifter behind.

"We'll soon be out of here," declared Elenna, tightening the coil of rope around her waist. "And the sooner, the better."

"It was a hard Quest," said Tom. "But we won in the end."

"And we've got back the first piece of the amulet for your father," said Elenna with a grin. "I know we've got five more to go but it's a good start."

"My father looked stronger already when he appeared to us just now, didn't he?" Tom asked eagerly.

Elenna nodded.

Tom felt a surge of happiness. He had grown up not knowing whether his father, Taladon, was alive or dead, but two days ago Tom had come face-to-face with him. He'd discovered that his father was a ghost stranded between the real world and the spirit realm. Malvel's evil magic had done this, and the only way to make Taladon flesh and blood again was to locate the six pieces of the Amulet of Avantia and fit them all together. This was Tom's Quest, but it would not be easy to recover the amulet fragments because each one was guarded by one of Malvel's Ghost Beasts.

Tom touched the first piece of the amulet that

hung from the leather cord around his neck. Taladon had told them that the second piece was guarded by Equinus the Spirit Horse.

"Father said Equinus would be a dangerous foe," Tom commented. "But we won't let that stop us."

"No, we won't," Elenna said determinedly. "Look, we're leaving the mines at last!" They ran out of the tunnel.

As they blinked in the sunlight, they heard a friendly whinny and a happy bark. Storm, Tom's stallion, and Silver, Elenna's wolf, came charging over to them.

"Thank you for waiting so patiently," Tom said to Storm as he stroked the horse's glossy black neck.

"I think they're glad to see us!" Elenna laughed. Silver was jumping around her in circles, barking excitedly.

"Now that the team's all together, we can start our next Quest." Tom held out his hand. "Map," he called.

The air in front of them shimmered and the map that Aduro had given to Tom materialized. They would have to fight Ghost Beasts—so the map itself was ghostly. It hung in the air before them, showing the whole dusty, gray Forbidden Land.

"We're here." Elenna pointed to the rocky mouth of the mine on the map.

"And that's the way we must go!" exclaimed Tom, as a glowing path appeared that led in a straight line across the map and into a tangled knot of trees. "To that forest in the east." Tom stared at the trees on the map. They looked dark and forbidding. He knew that somewhere among those trunks lurked Equinus.

Tom flicked open the brass lid of the compass that his father had given him. He did not need to look to remember the words inscribed on the bottom: *For My Son*. They always filled him with a warm glow. He located east on the navigational instrument and pointed in that direction. "We have a long journey ahead of us," he said. "It'll be quicker if we ride." He swung up onto Storm's back and held out a hand to Elenna.

"The beginning of another adventure!" cried Elenna as she climbed up behind him. She sounded excited but Tom could sense that she had the same fears as he did. The two friends had already met many fearsome and terrifying Beasts on their Quests.

What new terrors awaited them now?